JUL 2002

E+
Ryl

Rylant,
Cynthia.
The
High-Rise
Private Eyes :
the case of
the

SEP 0 3 2002
SEP 1 1 2002
OCT - 2 2002
DEC 2 8 2002
FEB 4 2003
APR 1 3 2003
JUN 2 3 2003
JUL 1 0 2003
SEP 1 9 2003
SEP 2 8 2003

WITHDRAWN
Woodridge Public Library

WOODRIDGE PUBLIC LIBRARY
3 PLAZA DRIVE
WOODRIDGE, IL 60517-5014
(630) 964-7899

In a high-rise building
deep in the heart of a big city
live two private eyes:
Bunny Brown and Jack Jones.
Bunny is the brains,
Jack is the snoop,
and together they
crack cases wide open . . .

This is the story of
Case Number 004:
THE CASE OF
THE TROUBLESOME TURTLE.

story by
Cynthia Rylant
pictures by
G. Brian Karas

WOODRIDGE PUBLIC LIBRARY
3 PLAZA DRIVE
WOODRIDGE, IL 60517-5014
(630) 964-7899

To Samantha Wills

—C. R.

To the Chancellor Livingston School

—G. B. K.

The High-Rise Private Eyes: The Case of the Troublesome Turtle
Text copyright © 2001 by Cynthia Rylant
Illustrations copyright © 2001 by G. Brian Karas
All rights reserved.
Printed in Hong Kong
by South China Printing Company (1988) Ltd.
www.harperchildrens.com

Acrylic, gouache, and pencil were used for the full-color art.
The text type is Times.

Library of Congress Cataloging-in-Publication Data
Rylant, Cynthia.
The high-rise private eyes : the case of the troublesome turtle /
by Cynthia Rylant ; illustrated by G. Brian Karas.
p. cm.
"Greenwillow Books."
Summary: Bunny and Jack, animal detectives,
investigate the disappearance of the balloons
from the neighborhood toy store.
ISBN 0-688-16312-2 (trade)
ISBN 0-688-16311-4 (lib. bdg.)
[1. Animals—Fiction. 2. Balloons—Fiction.
3. Football—Fiction. 4. Mystery and detective stories.]
I. Karas, G. Brian, ill. II. Title.
PZ7.R982Hq 2001 [E]—dc21 00-044271

3 4 5 6 7 8 9 10

Contents

BIG GAME!

Bunny enjoyed painting on Sundays.

"Why don't you paint me?"

asked Jack.

"Because you won't sit still,"

said Bunny.

"Yes, I will," said Jack.

"No, you won't," said Bunny.

"Will," said Jack.

"Won't," said Bunny.

"Let's just *try,*" said Jack.

"I'll be as still as that apple."

"Oh, all right," said Bunny.

"Just sit on that chair there.

And don't move."

"Goody," said Jack.

He sat on the chair.

Bunny began to paint.

"Uh-oh," said Jack.

"What?" asked Bunny.

"My nose itches," said Jack.

"Don't scratch," said Bunny.

"Okay," said Jack.

He didn’t scratch.

But he turned all red from wanting to.

Bunny kept painting.

“Uh-oh,” said Jack again.

“What?” asked Bunny.

“Now my chin itches,” said Jack.

“Don’t scratch,” said Bunny.

“Okay,” said Jack.

He didn’t scratch.

But his eyes bugged out

from wanting to.

Bunny kept painting.

“Uh-oh,” said Jack a third time.

“What now?” asked Bunny.

“Now my toe itches,” said Jack.

“Don’t scratch,” said Bunny.

"Okay," said Jack.
He didn't scratch.
But his fur stood on end
from wanting to.

Finally Bunny was finished.
"Okay, all done," she said.
"Thank goodness," said Jack,
scratching like crazy.
"I was about to scream."
"Silly," said Bunny.

"Can I see?" asked Jack.

"Sure," said Bunny.

Jack looked at the painting.

"AAAAGGGGHHHHH!" Jack screamed.

"Goodness," said Bunny.

"Do I really look like that?"

asked Jack.

"Only if you need to scratch,"
said Bunny.
"I never knew
how important scratching is,"
said Jack.
"I'm going to scratch more often."
"Okay," said Bunny.
"Five times a day," said Jack.
"Fine," said Bunny.

"Now I know why you
  like to paint apples," said Jack.

"Why?" asked Bunny.

"Because they don't itch," said Jack.

"Bingo," said Bunny.

"I will never ask you
  to paint me again," said Jack.

"Okay," said Bunny.

“But could you scratch my back?”
asked Jack.
“Right here, where I can’t reach?”
“Oh, for goodness’ sake,” said Bunny.

Chapter 2
The Case

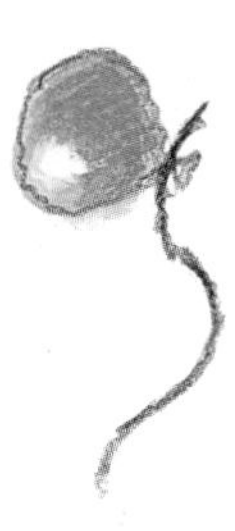

Bunny and Jack were just about to go out to lunch when someone knocked on Bunny's door. It was Mr. Paris, who owned the toy store across the street.

"Hello, Mr. Paris!" said Bunny.

"Hello, Bunny. Hello, Jack,"
said Mr. Paris. "I think I need
a private eye. Somebody keeps
taking my balloons."

"Come in," said Bunny.
"Tell us about it."

She grabbed her notepad.
“Which balloons? Where?”
asked Jack.
“The ones I tie
to the front of the store,”
said Mr. Paris,
sitting down.

"I always tie four balloons outside
in the morning.
And somebody keeps taking them."
"Hmmm," said Bunny.
She wrote down:

4 balloons outside

"What do the balloons look like?"

Bunny asked.

"They're green and yellow,"

said Mr. Paris,

"to match my delivery truck.

And they're tied with blue ribbon."

Bunny wrote down:

green and yellow
blue ribbon

"And do they disappear every day?"

she asked.

"No—only on Fridays,"

said Mr. Paris.

"Hmmm," said Bunny.

She wrote down:

disappear on Fridays

"And when did this start happening?"
Bunny asked.

"This fall," said Mr. Paris.

"No one ever bothered them
in the summer."

"Hmmm," said Bunny again.
She wrote down:

fall, not summer

"And do you have any
Android Attack action figures?"
asked Jack.

"What's that got to do
with anything?" asked Bunny.

"Nothing," said Jack.
"I just like them."

"Concentrate on the case, Jack," said Bunny.

"Right," said Jack. "Mr. Paris, on your way through the store to tie up the balloons, which are now missing, did you ever pass any Android Attack action figures?"

"Jack!" said Bunny.

"What?" asked Jack.

"Mr. Paris," said Bunny, "don't worry.
We'll solve this case.
You can count on us."
She gave Jack a look.
"Well, one of us will, anyway," she said.
"Hey," said Jack.

"Thank you, Bunny. Thank you, Jack,"

said Mr. Paris.

"I knew I could depend on you."

Mr. Paris walked to the door.

"By the way, Jack," he said,

"I have seven

Android Attack action figures.

And they come with accessories."

"COOL!" said Jack.

Bunny just sighed.

"Okay," said Bunny
after Mr. Paris left.
"Let's look at our clues."
"Okay," said Jack.
They read the clues.
"Green and yellow.
Blue ribbon.
Fridays in the fall," said Bunny.
"TGIF," said Jack.
"What?" asked Bunny.

“‘Thank goodness it’s Friday,’”
said Jack. “TGIF.
Didn’t you say that
when you were in school?”
“No,” said Bunny. “I said,
‘Gee, I have a ton of homework.’”

"Oh," said Jack. "Too bad.

I said it.

Because Fridays meant fun.

Movies, cookouts, ball games,

swim—"

"WAIT!" said Bunny. "THAT'S IT!"

"What's it?" asked Jack.

"Ball games," said Bunny.

"In the fall. On Fridays."

Jack thought a minute.

"Right!" he said. "And just as
Mr. Paris wants colors
that match his truck, . . ."

"School kids want colors
that match their team," said Bunny.

"I'll bet somebody
is taking those balloons
to Friday night football games."

"Right," said Jack.

"Let's think about school colors,"
said Bunny.

"There's the Westover Weasels."

"Red and gray," said Jack.

"The Southside Seagulls."

"Blue and white," said Jack.

"And the Tarrytown Turtles."

"GREEN AND YELLOW!"
said Jack.

"Bingo," said Bunny.

"We're going to a game."

"Yay, team!" said Jack.

TURTLES!

Chapter 4
Solved

Jack picked up Bunny
on Friday night.
He was wearing a turtle shirt,
a turtle hat,
and a turtle scarf.
He also had a pom-pom.
"We have to fit in,"
said Jack.
"Right," said Bunny.

"Do you want the hat?" asked Jack.

"No," said Bunny.

"The scarf?"

"No," said Bunny.

"Well, you can't have the shirt," said Jack. "I'll catch cold."

"I want the pom-pom," said Bunny.

“But the pom-pom’s the most fun,”
said Jack. “I thought
you’d want the hat.”
“Let’s share the pom-pom,”
said Bunny.
“Okay,” said Jack.
“I get it first.”

Football
Field

"No, me," said Bunny.

"Me," said Jack.

"Jack, you said you'd share,"
said Bunny.

"I have trouble
sharing pom-poms," said Jack.

"Oh, all right," said Bunny.
"I'll wear the hat."

She put it on.
“Bunny, you look MARVELOUS!”
said Jack.
“Ha,” said Bunny.

Jack and Bunny went to see
the Tarrytown Turtles play
the Southside Seagulls.
They sat on the Turtles' side.
Everything was green and yellow,
including four balloons.

“Look!” said Jack.

A young turtle was holding
the balloons and cheering.

“How do we know they belong
to Mr. Paris?” asked Jack.

“Mr. Paris said he tied them together
with blue ribbon,”
said Bunny.

“Let’s go see,” said Jack.

They stood behind the turtle.
"Bingo," said Bunny.
"Now what?" asked Jack.
"Well," said Bunny.
"He's just a kid.
We don't want to scare him
or make him cry."
"Right," said Jack. "Wow,
do you smell that popcorn?"
"That's *it*!" said Bunny.
"Oh, good, I'm starving," said Jack.
"No, I mean we'll use *popcorn*.
We'll write a note and stick it
in a popcorn cup," said Bunny.
"Great," said Jack. "You write the note
while I get the popcorn. It's my *JOB*!"
"Ha," said Bunny.

While Jack got three cups of popcorn, Bunny wrote a little note. It said:

Please don't take balloons
from the toy store,
or you know what.
Santa Claus

Jack and Bunny gave the young turtle their extra cup of popcorn.

Then they left.

"What did the note say?"
asked Jack.

"It said 'This raccoon eats too much,' "
said Bunny.

"Very funny," said Jack.

"By the way, are you hungry?
Want to get another snack?"

"Well, I have some apples at home,"
said Bunny.

"You mean the kind that don't itch?"
asked Jack.

"Yes," said Bunny.

"Cool," said Jack.

On the way home
Bunny and Jack rode past
Mr. Paris's store.
A nice young turtle
was tying some balloons
to the door.
"Case closed," said Bunny.
"TGIF," said Jack.
"What?" asked Bunny.

“Thank goodness I’m fantastic,”
said Jack.

“Silly,” said Bunny.

“You bet!” said Jack.

3 1524 00355 4005